En camino a comprar huevos

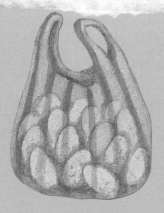

Escrito e ilustrado por

Chih-Yuan Chen

Kane/Miller
BOOK PUBLISHERS

– ¿Puedo salir a jugar? –pregunta Shau-yu.

– Necesito que vayas a la tienda primero –contesta su papá.
– No tenemos huevos.

Shau-yu pone el dinero en el bolsillo derecho de su falda.
(No hay agujeros en ese bolsillo.)

Afuera, sigue la sombra del gato. El gato anda por el techo.

Ella espía a la vuelta del muro. – guau guau – ladra como un perro,

justo como Harry siempre lo hace.

Levanta una canica perdida.
Es azul, el color del ojo del gato.

Mirando por el ojo azul...

Las ventanas son azules; los muros son azules.
Las casas son azules; el cielo es azul.
El mundo se vuelve un mundo azul como el mar.

– Soy un pequeño pez, nadando en
el gran mar azul.
(Shau-yu quiere decir "pequeño pez".)

Pisando en hojas caídas del árbol
–Chi-cha, chi-cha– Los pasos de
Shau-yu suenan como cuando se
come galletas crocantes.

Bajo el árbol encuentra unas gafas que parece que están pidiendo que alguien se las ponga.

Shau-yu se parece a su Mamá ahora.

Todo parece borroso.

Es un mundo borroso.

Pero Shau-yu conoce el camino.

Ahí está la tienda, allá, cerca a aquel poste.

– Hola, señor. Quisiera comprar huevos por favor, huevos para preparar arroz frito. Voy a cocinar arroz frito y huevos por mi familia esta noche.

– Aquí están sus huevos, Señora. ¿Tal vez su hijita, Shau-yu, quisiera un chicle?

– Ummm. Creo que sí.

– ¿Pone el huevo primero la gallina?

– ¿o sale el pollito del cascarón? –Se pregunta Shau-yu.

Shau-yu se fija en dos flores hermosas
en la esquina del muro.

El agua en sus pétalos brilla como
los diamantes.

– Debería llevar estas flores a casa –piensa ella.

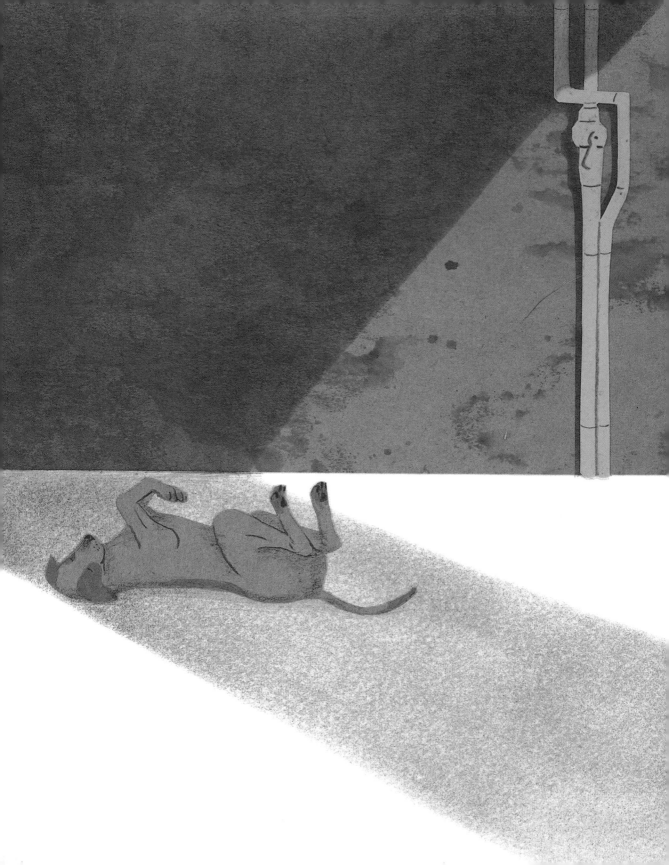

El chicle ya ha perdido su sabor. Pero, todavía sirve para hacer globos.

¡Pop!

Despierta a Harry como mágica.

Din, don.
– ¡Hola! Mi día fue muy ocupado.

El Premio "Hsin Yi Picture Book" fue establecido en 1987 para alentar a los autores e ilustradores taiwaneses a crear libros chinos ilustrados de alta calidad para niños.

En camino a comprar huevos ganó el premio en 1997. Los jueces sintieron que este libro iba "hacer sentir a los niños que hay felicidad, humor y calidad sin fin en sus vidas diarias."

Painting **Flowers** *In Watercolor*

JOSE M. PARRAMON

Watson-Guptill Publications/New York

Copyright © 1989 by Parramón Ediciones, S.A.

First published in 1990 in the United States by Watson-Guptill
Publications, a division of BPI Communications, Inc.,
1515 Broadway, New York, New York 10036.

Library of Congress Cataloging-in-Publication Data

Parramón, José María.
    [Pintando flores a la acuarela. English]
    Painting flowers in watercolor / José M. Parramón.
        p.   cm.—(Watson-Guptill painting library)
    Translation of: Pintando flores a la acuarela.
    ISBN: 0-8230-1852-0 (paperback)
        1. Flowers in art. 2. Watercolor painting—Technique.
    I. Title. II. Series.
    ND2244. P3713 1990
    751.42'2434—dc20   90-12552
                                                                  CIP

Distributed in the United Kingdom by Phaidon Press Ltd.,
Musterlin House, Jordan Hill Road, Oxford OX2 8DP.

Manufactured in Spain
Legal Deposit: B-21.566-90

1 2 3 4 5 6 7 8 9 / 94 93 92 91 90

Painting **Flowers** *In Watercolor*

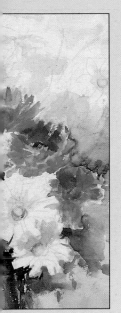  

The Watson-Guptill Painting Library is a collection of books aimed at guiding the painting and drawing student through the works of several professional artists. Each book demonstrates the various techniques, materials, and procedures used to paint in specific mediums, such as watercolor, acrylic, pastel, colored pencil, oil, and so on. Each book also focuses on a specific theme: landscape, nature, still life, figure, portrait, seascape, and so on. There is an explanatory introduction in each book in the series followed by lessons in drawing or painting the specific subject matter. In the introduction of this book, you will start by looking at different approaches to lighting, composition, and color harmony when painting flowers, as well as the crucial watercolor technique of saving blank spaces for light-colored forms.

Perhaps the most extraordinary aspect of this book is the way in which the lessons (the choice of subject matter; the composition; the color interpretation and harmony; the effects of light and shade; and the technical knowledge and experience along with the secrets and tricks provided by several professional artists) are explained and illustrated line by line, brushstroke by brushstroke, step by step, with dozens of photographs taken while the artists were creating their paintings.

I personally directed this series with a team that I am proud of, and I honestly believe this series can really teach you how to paint.

José M. Parramón

Introduction to the floral theme

More than a thousand years ago Chinese artists of the Sung dynasty were already painting flowers by combining black washes of Chinese ink with watercolors. This traditional Oriental theme and technique continues to be used by the majority of Chinese and Japanese artists to this very day.

In Western civilization paintings of plants and flowers first appeared in the houses of ancient Greece and Rome. There, however, they were used merely as ornamental motifs to decorate the walls of mansions such as those in Palatine and in Pompeii.

Flowers and plants were also used as a motif to adorn the manuscripts and codices of the Middle Ages in miniature. The first Western painting to have flowers as the actual subject was painted in oil five hundred years ago, in 1490, by the Flemish artist Hans Memling. *Vase of Flowers in a Niche* was painted in the city of Bruges, the capital of western Flanders, where Memling had lived since his early youth. We can say that this was the first real oil painting of flowers; oil painting was invented —or, more accurately, perfected— by the Flemish school

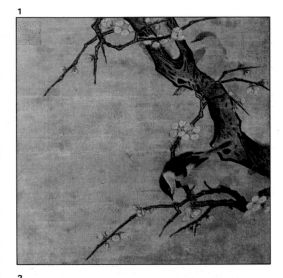

Fig. 1. Painting attributed to Ma Lin. *Birds and Plum Tree Flowers*, Goto Museum, Tokyo. The theme of flowers and birds has been traditional in China and Japan for more than a thousand years. Watercolors were being used even then.

Fig. 2. Hans Memling (1435-1494). *Vase of Flowers in a Niche*, Thyssen Collection, Lugano. This is the first recorded painting of flowers in the history of Western art. It is probably the first oil painting of flowers painted by Memling, a member of the Flemish school.

Fig. 3. Albrecht Dürer (1471-1528). *Fleur-de-lis* or *Iris*. Since Dürer was the first Western painter to use watercolors, we can assume that this is one of the first paintings of flowers done in watercolor.

4

5

founded by Jan van Eyck, of which Memling was a member.

In Nuremberg five years later, in 1495, Albrecht Dürer painted the first watercolor painting of flowers, *Fleur-de-lis* (fig. 3). Dürer was to become the most famous German painter and engraver of the sixteenth century, and he painted a total of 188 pictures, eighty-six of which were watercolors. He treated his watercolor landscapes, animals, and flowers as completed works even though at that time watercolors were considered to be mere preliminary studies for oil paintings.

Memling and the Flemish school were responsible for popularizing paintings of flowers. This group of artists spanned from

the seventeenth to the eighteenth century and included such painters as Jan Brueghel, Bosschaert, Rubens, and later Jan van Huysum. Their work influenced the development of as well as the demand for pictures of flowers in Germany, Italy, and France. This was the era during which the works of Monnoyer, Desportes, Roland de la Porte, Anne Vallayer-Coster, and the great Jean-Baptiste-Siméon Chardin triumphed in France.

During the nineteenth century, most artists painted flowers at least periodically. Their ranks include Constable, Lewis, Delacroix, Feuerbach, Courbet, and, of course, the impressionists.

Fig. 4. Jan Brueghel (1568-1625). *Large Bouquet of Flowers in a Vase,* Alte Pinakothek, Munich. Brueghel was one of the Flemish artists who specialized in painting flowers. He was so highly respected that he sometimes painted the ornamental flower crowns and wreaths of Rubens's Madonnas and Virgins.

Fig. 5. Anne Vallayer-Coster (1744-1818). *Flowers in a Blue Porcelain Vase,* private collection, Paris.

Monet's flowers

Monet, Cézanne, Degas, Pissarro, Renoir, Manet, van Gogh... all the impressionists and postimpressionists painted pictures of flowers, some as famous as van Gogh's sunflowers or Monet's great water lilies series. The story of this series of paintings illustrates Monet's perfectionism.

In 1883 Claude Monet rented a house — which was later to become his— in a town called Giverny on the banks of the Seine River, between Paris and Rouen. In his garden Monet built a lake under a bridge that stood next to several summer pavilions and filled the water with hundreds of floating water lilies in full bloom to create the effect of a Japanese water garden. Building on this theme —the garden, the lake, the water lilies— by 1890, Monet had painted numerous pictures and studies in which he tried to portray, in his own words, "the mirror of water, the constant changes in the surface caused by the reflections of bits of sky that endow the lake with life and movement."

6

On the basis of these studies, Monet's friend Georges Clemenceau (the Minister and President of the French government during World War I) commissioned Monet to paint nineteen large paintings of the lake and water lilies in 1916. These were to be housed in the two great exhibition halls of L'Orangerie in the Tuilleries.

The official act donating the work to the French government was signed on April 12, 1922, but Monet never stopped. He kept on painting, repainting, and perfecting; he doubted the value of his work. Clemenceau then wrote to him, "You are being absolutely ridiculous when you say you are not sure that the works you are going to give me are worthwhile. You know very well that you have reached the limits of the attainable. But I understand your doubts: if you weren't forever pushing yourself to find something even better, you wouldn't have been the creator of so many masterpieces that are the pride of France."

Fig. 6. Claude Monet (1840-1926). *Pond with Water Lilies*, Museum of Fine Art, Caen. This is but a fragment of his famous series of nineteen paintings of aquatic plants and their reflection in the lake at Giverny.

Van Gogh's flowers

Van Gogh and his flower paintings are another good example of an artist's struggle to improve his work.

In February of 1888 Vincent van Gogh left Paris to travel to Arles, a city in the southern French region of Provence, where he lived for fourteen months. During this time he painted close to two hundred paintings and drew more than a hundred drawings. Van Gogh, like many artists, painted the same theme over and over again: Rembrandt painted more than sixty self-portraits and Cézanne made fifty-five pictures of Mount Sainte-Victoire. While in Arles, van Gogh painted five self-portraits, three pictures of his room, and seven pictures of sunflowers.

In May of 1890 van Gogh was admitted to the mental asylum of Saint-Rémy. It was there, in the asylum garden, that he painted his picture *Irises*. One year later —just two months before committing suicide— he painted irises again. There is only one possible explanation for this repetition of theme: the desire to learn, to practice, to study.

This is the lesson to be learned from Monet and van Gogh: you have to study, you have to persevere, you have to practice constantly by drawing and painting many sketches, many color studies, and many flowers. This is the only way to perfect your painting and succeed in producing a good work of art.

Figs. 7 to 11. *Fourteen Sunflowers in a Vase*, Tate Gallery, London (fig. 7); *The Sunflowers*, Vincent van Gogh Foundation, National Vincent van Gogh Museum, Amsterdam (fig. 8); *Vase with Fourteen Sunflowers*, private collection, London (fig. 9); *Vase of Purple Irises with Yellow Background*, Vincent van Gogh Foundation, National Vincent van Gogh Museum, Amsterdam (fig. 10); *Irises*, private collection (fig. 11). During his stay in Arles van Gogh painted seven pictures of sunflowers. The following year he painted two pictures of irises in Saint-Rémy. The picture in figure 10 was painted two months before he committed suicide. Of the close to 250 paintings that van Gogh produced in Arles, he only sold one *(Red Vineyards of Arles)* for 400 francs. Now van Gogh's works are fetching the highest prices ever paid in the history of art.

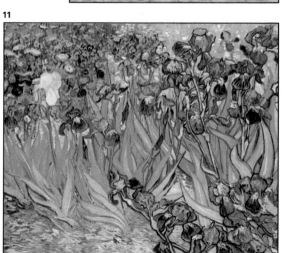

Materials needed for painting in watercolor

An easel is not absolutely necessary for watercolors; a notebook or a plywood board will do (a). Paper is the support (b) and there are no solvents other than water (c). Also needed are a natural sponge (d), a rag or roll of paper towels (e), metal clips or tacks to attach the paper to the board (f), and a palette (g). Only two brushes are really necessary: a round number 12 or 14 sable brush (h) and a flat ¾-inch (2-cm) fitch-hair or synthetic fiber brush (i), although of course you can work better if you have a wider variety of brushes that includes a flat Japanese hake (j), a number 8 sable brush (k), and a brush with a bevel-edged handle for opening up blank spaces (l).

Besides this you need a soft lead pencil (m), an eraser (n), a pencil sharpener (o), and two special substances for reserving white spaces: liquid drawing gum, or frisket, (p), or an artist's oil crayon (q). The drawing gum is applied with an old or low-quality brush to the spaces to be left blank. Let the gum dry, paint watercolor over it, and remove the gum with an eraser to expose white paper below. The same effect can be achieved with strokes of the oil crayon.

Last are the watercolors themselves. They can take the liquid form (r) often used in illustration and airbrush painting; the moist form in pans (s) placed in metal boxes that serve as palettes (t); or cream in tubes (u), to be used with a palette similiar to the one on page 9. Speaking of palettes, it's also possible to use plastic pans.

That's all you'll need. Well, almost all. For studio painting the water container should be wide-necked. For outdoor painting it's convenient to have a plastic container as well as a plastic bottle for transporting the water.

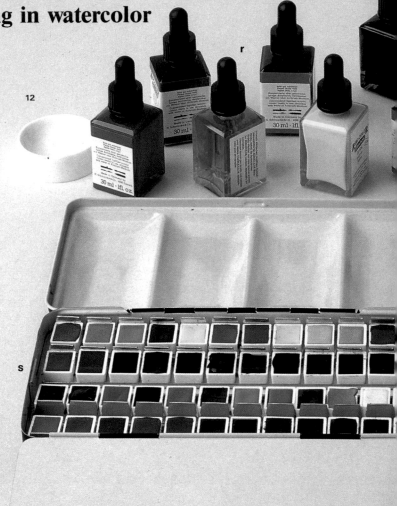

9

"One paints as one draws."—Ingres

"One paints as one draws." With this sentence Ingres summarized the necessity of knowing how to draw and doing it extensively in order to paint well. Painting is drawing. This is especially valid in the case of watercolor painting, in which the artist has to draw the form of a flower or leaf with paint. In the case of a daisy, for example, you must outline the petals with a dark color so as to define its white space. Much drawing and sketching, studying, and memorizing of forms is required in order to be able to draw and paint at the same time.

You have to study. Take notes and draw flowers. Flowers, like all other objects, can be drawn by modifying a basic geometric shape, as shown by the illustrations on this page. Practice this drawing technique whenever you sketch flowers outdoors. It is indispensable for successful watercolor painting.

13

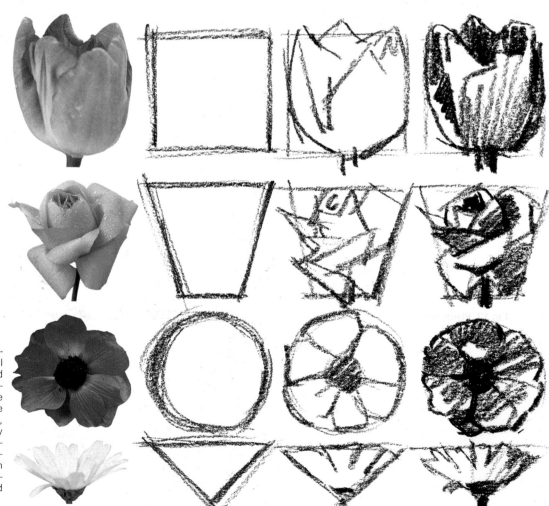

Fig. 13. Flowers are no exception to the rule that all objects can be structured and drawn from basic geometric shapes such as the square, the rectangle, the truncated cone, the circle, and the triangle. I highly recommend that you practice this exercise by sketching —from nature, from photographs, or from illustrations in books and magazines.

Figs. 14 to 17. Plants and flowers, just like other subjects, demand exhaustive knowledge on the part of the artist about form and color, structure and texture, the effect of the direction of light and the time of day, and so on. This can be learned only by drawing, painting, and, above all, sketching many flowers whether indoors or outdoors. All you need is a block of drawing paper and a soft lead pencil, such as 6B.

"To make a study is to make a picture."—van Gogh

18

19

What applies to drawing and sketching also applies to painting sketches and color studies before painting the actual picture.

Helmut Ruheman is a writer, an artist, and chief restorer of the National Gallery of London. In one of his books he explains that he spent two years working in Paris with Maurice Denis. "I'll never forget his best piece of advice: before beginning a painting, paint a rapid stamp-sized sketch, and then whatever you do, don't abandon this first spontaneous idea."

If you are thinking of painting flowers, I recommend that you dedicate some work sessions entirely to recording impressions and painting rapid sketches. As van Gogh commented to his brother Theo on sketching and taking notes, "To my mind, to make a study is to sow; to make pictures, to reap."

Figs. 21 to 26. Watercolor paint is transparent rather than opaque. Consequently spaces have to be reserved or left white wherever light-colored forms are desired. It's also possible to use liquid drawing gum, a grayish solution that keeps the paper white while you paint over and around it. When you are finally ready to expose the white paper, remove the liquid drawing gum. You can then leave that area white or paint it a light color.

20

Figs. 18 to 20. Quick sketches and color studies are the best exercises for learning how to paint flowers —or any other subject, for that matter—and for perfecting your watercolor technique. These color sketches are, as van Gogh said, "the seed that permits us to reap good pictures."

Saved blank space: A basic factor in watercolor painting

As you know, there is no white watercolor paint; the only white is the white of the paper. Watercolor is a transparent medium. This means that to achieve light colors and whites you have to leave spaces empty and thus take advantage of the transparent paint and the white of the paper.

To make it easier to leave spaces blank or white, some watercolorists use the liquid drawing gum mentioned earlier, which we illustrate in the following pictures.

27

28

Figs. 27 and 28. In these two images, note the use of the saved blank space in portraying light-colored flowers against a dark background. This is a technique characteristic of watercolor painting.

The setup: Arranging your flowers

29

30

31

The easiest part of being a flower painter is finding and arranging flowers. There are flowers in the countryside, in gardens, in flowerpots on terraces or inside houses, and —in great quantity and diversity— in florists' shops: fresh flowers, dried flowers, real flowers, artificial flowers. The latter can only be used if they are of high quality.

Arrange your bouquet of flowers yourself since you will no doubt be more discerning than the store clerk when it comes to placement and composition. Very thin wire comes in handy for winding around stems. That way you can lengthen the stem of a flower in a vase to make it stand taller or straighten the stem of a wilted flower (fig. 33).

32

33

Figs. 29 to 31. Flowers are easy to find in gardens, growing wild, and in florists' shops. It's even possible to use artificial flowers such as the ones in figure 31.

Fig. 32. Prepare and arrange your own bouquet of flowers since you have your own criteria for composition.

Fig. 33. Wire is useful for modifying the length of a stem, keeping a flower in a specific position, and reinforcing the stem of a slightly wilted flower.

Lighting and contrast

34

35

36

Before beginning to paint your flower picture, study all the lighting possibilities and choose the most appropriate one by taking into account the color and shape of the bouquet, the vase, the background, and so on.

The different possibilities can be summed up by two different qualities of light and three different directional positionings of light:

Direct light: This is the quality of light coming directly from the sun or from an artificial spotlight. It causes deep shadows and accentuates color contrasts.

Diffuse or scattered light: This is light on a cloudy day, or indirect light coming from a window usually located above floor level.

Frontal illumination: The light is directly in front of the setup, so there are no shadows. This is perfect for coloristic style painting.

Frontal-lateral illumination: This is the most commonly used position: partway between the front and the side. Its interplay of light and dark best defines the volume and form of objects.

Backlighting: Light comes from behind the model thus darkening everything and throwing a classic halo around objects. If you soften the shadows with a reflecting panel or screen, you can obtain some very artistic lighting.

Figs. 34 to 36. The effects of light and shadow of the three classic lighting positions: frontal lighting, lateral lighting, and backlighting.

Figs. 37 and 38. The law of simultaneous contrasts says that a color looks lighter when a dark color surrounds it, and vice versa.

Fig. 39. The juxtaposition of two complementary colors, in this case green and red, causes maximum color contrast.

37

38

39

Color contrast can be influenced by two basic factors:

Simultaneous contrast: The lighter the color surrounding another color, the darker the surrounded color will appear. Conversely, the darker the surrounding color, the lighter seems the surrounded color.

Juxtaposition of complementary colors: Complementary colors placed close together look extraordinarily intense. For example, try juxtaposing red with green, yellow with dark blue (ultramarine), or red with medium blue (viridian).

Composition: Symmetry, asymmetry

40

41

42

One of the most commonly used compositional formats is that of symmetry, which is characterized by the equal distribution of pictorial elements on both sides of a central axis. The bouquet of flowers and vase placed in the exact middle of Chardin's famous painting (fig. 40) corresponds to this compositional format, which is the one most frequently used in painting flowers. However, while maintaining this basic symmetrical format, it is possible to make slight variations by adding objects to one or both sides of the flower vase as Francesc Crespo did (fig. 42). If we want to compose more freely and move from symmetry to asymmetry, it's necessary to place the flowers and vase to one side of the picture so that they form part of a whole. Most asymmetrical compositions contain many objects that provide variety without losing unity or distracting attention from the subject of the painting. As an example of this, we have a splendid watercolor of a bouquet by the American artist Charles Reid (fig. 41). Achieving variety within unity and unity within variety is the basic concept underlying good composition.

Figs. 40 to 42. Jean-Baptiste-Simeón Chardin (1699-1779). *Flowers in a Blue Vase*, National Gallery of Scotland, Edinburgh. Charles Reid, *Tabletop and Flowers*, private collection. Francesc Crespo, *Flowers*, private collection.

Color harmony

43

44

45

COLOR RANGES

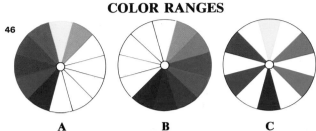

46

| A | B | C |

Any painting is much more pleasant and attractive when its tones and hues go well together. The spectrum of colors can be divided into three basic ranges:

The warm color range (fig. 43).
The cool color range (fig. 44).
The neutral color range (fig. 45).

The color range in question is usually determined by the colors of the flowers themselves or by the means of lighting. In the studio during the morning of a clear and sunny day, the light has a bluish tendency; it leans toward cool colors. In that same studio after four or five o'clock in the afternoon, the light will turn orangish and the tendency will be toward warm colors. On a gray, cloudy day, colors will tend toward gray and fall within the range of neutral or dirty colors. Artificial incandescent light is yellow, warm; fluorescent light can be blue, cool.

From an artistic point of view what is important is that you see this tendency and accentuate it while trying to achieve the best possible color harmony. Look at the three adjacent details of watercolor paintings of flowers that illustrate the three color ranges or tendencies. From top to bottom, they are: *warm range, cool range,* and *neutral range.*

Those are the basics. In the following pages you'll see how our guest artists paint. I hope you will also paint your own pictures and experience that wonderful adventure known as painting flowers in watercolor.

Fig. 46A. The warm color range consists predominately of yellows, oranges, reds, and so on.

Fig. 46B. The cool color range is made up mostly of greens, blues, violets, and so on.

Fig. 46C. The neutral color range contains colors with a tendency towards gray, the result of mixing complementary colors with white.

Guillem Fresquet: A veteran expert

Guillem Fresquet is going to paint a bouquet of flowers in watercolor. He is an expert artist capable of dealing with any theme, be it landscape, seascape, the human figure, or flowers. (A few of his watercolor paintings are reproduced on this page.)

"Have you always painted with watercolors?" I ask.

Fresquet is holding up a drawing board to which a large medium-grain sheet of Arches watercolor paper is attached by just four tacks. "Yes, always. Though in the beginning, when I started to paint, I did also practice with oils. But I soon understood that watercolor could much more rapidly capture a momentary impression. The atmosphere of a cloudy day, the warm feeling of an autumn landscape, even the movement of human figures can be caught only with a rapid sketch and with a medium as fast-drying and easy to set up as watercolors."

"I see that you don't mount your paper according to the traditional system of wetting it and then stretching it out and attaching it to the drawing board with strips of masking tape."

"I almost never do that," responds Fresquet as he sets up his colors, water, and brushes. "If the paper is like this, thick and of good quality, there's no need to do that."

47

Figs. 47 to 52. Guillem Fresquet, whom we see in the top photograph, is an expert in watercolor, capable of painting anything from landscapes and seascapes to human figures and flowers.

48

49

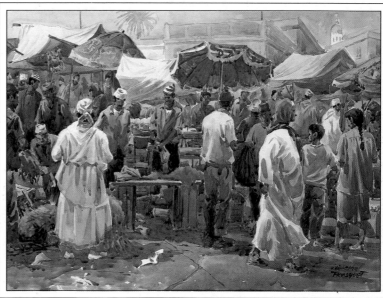

Guillem Fresquet's works

50

51

52

The materials and the drawing

Figs. 53 and 54. Fresquet recently traveled to Morocco, where he painted a series of watercolor landscapes with people. These paintings demonstrate his extraordinary capacity to combine the human figure with other subjects.

Fig. 55. Here you see tools currently being used by Fresquet for watercolor painting: creamy tube paints, sable brushes, flat brushes for wetting wide areas, a pencil, an eraser, a rag to absorb water and clean brushes, and two water containers (one containing a teaspoonful of sugar to slow down watercolor drying time). This helps avoid any sharp edges or irregularities in the background.

53

54

55

You can see the materials used by Fresquet in figure 55: a metal palette for creamy tube watercolors; several sable brushes of varying sizes, although Fresquet actually uses only a number 14 brush, a number 7 brush, and a 2-inch (5 cm) flat hake brush; a pencil, an eraser, and a piece of cloth; a rag to absorb and drain water from the brushes; and two containers of water, with a level teaspoon of sugar added to one of them. "It's an old trick for slowing down how fast the watercolors dry," explains Fresquet as I take note.

56

57

Fig. 56. This setup consists of a ceramic vase full of daisies, carnations, and calendulas against a background of blue cloth and light-colored wood.

Figs. 57 and 58. Fresquet's sketch is best characterized as a linear drawing that merely situates the compositional elements of the picture. He usually wets the paper in order to eliminate any grease and to help the watercolors merge.

58

Fresquet composes and arranges the bouquet using the props you can see in figure 56. While our guest artist is determining the exact placement of the flowers —some a bit higher, some a bit lower— he comments, "I would say that a bouquet has to offer the appearance of 'loosely disordered order' in order to seem more real, more natural."

Once he is seated a few yards away from the flowers, with the bottom of the drawing board resting against his lap and the side being held up by his left hand, Fresquet draws them using a mechanical pencil with soft lead. The result is a rapid sketch consisting of short but definite strokes that suggest the forms in a few concise lines.

Next Fresquet dampens the paper with clean water, using his hake brush. "This is something I do as much to eliminate any remaining traces of grease as to apply the first colors to a wet surface, in an attempt to create a spontaneous finish from the very beginning," he says.

The first colors, the first flowers

Figs. 59 and 60. Fresquet begins to paint on the wet paper surface with his customary spontaneity and sureness of hand.

"See?" True to his own words, Fresquet applies a pink color to the wet surface where the red flower sticks out from the top of the bouquet. The color on his brush is immediately diluted by the wet paper. Using the same pink color, Fresquet paints the carnations on the upper left side with quick, precise touches.

Next, using his fattest brush (a number 14 sable), he adds a little more carmine to the pink and mixes it with yellow. He tries out a little of the color on the paper, and then returns to the palette to dirty it a bit. "It was too strident," he says. And now he paints the orange flowers in the middle of the bouquet, taking care to harmonize the bright colors with the dirty tones left over in the palette. Again, the color is diluted as it spreads over the surface of the paper, which is still slightly damp.

Observing the almost vertical position of the drawing board as Fresquet works, I can't help but think of the risk of trickles, drips, and smudges from momentarily overloading the brush with water. "Do you think many watercolorists paint with the drawing board in a nearly vertical position like you're doing now?"

"I suppose you're asking that because of the danger of trickling or dripping washes. Well, I don't really have a personal preference as to how much to incline the board. Sometimes in the countryside I paint with the board lying on the grass, in a totally horizontal position. In the studio I usually tilt the board 20 to 30 degrees. However, among professional painters, it's not at all unusual to paint with the drawing board mounted on a easel in an almost vertical or totally vertical position. Trickles and drips can be avoided if you're careful. If not... well, depending on how they drip, they can help create contrasts. Let me show you; I'm going to paint the background cloth right now to illustrate the problem."

59

60

Fig. 61. As you can see in this image, Fresquet paints with his paper on an almost vertical drawing board balanced against his lap, thus proving that it is possible to waterpaint without an easel. A notebook or plywood board will suffice.

61

62

63

64

Figs. 62 to 64. In these pictures you can see the synthesis of form and color with which Fresquet portrays the central calendulas. Also note the neutral green color of the first leaves, which was obtained by mixing an orange-red with an emerald green complementary to red.

Painting the background and leaving spaces for flowers

In watercolor painting, coloring the background presupposes reserving blank spaces destined to become lighter-colored forms. This is the most difficult part of watercolor painting, the part that requires great skill, total mastery of drawing, and an immediate grasp of dimensions and proportions in order to successfully combine forms as diverse as those of this bouquet.

This is what Guillem Fresquet is doing right now. With a number 14 brush in hand, he prepares a slightly dirty light blue wash in his palette by mixing Payne's gray with Prussian blue. Initially the separate brushstrokes stand out, but seconds later they blend as the color evens out. Fresquet removes the extra water that accumulates at the upper edges of his brush, using a rag he always has handy. He also uses a half-dry brush to absorb some, but not all, of the surplus wash from the paper. "In some places it's actually good to leave accumulations of wash and color, because once they dry, they outline and highlight the form or shape of the saved blank area." This is true and worth remembering; check to see how some of these pockets of wash and color (indicated by arrows in fig. 71) remain visible and serve to bring out contrasts in the finished watercolor, which you can see in figure 79 on page 29.

Figs. 65 to 72. Here we have a sequence of photographs taken as Fresquet was painting the background and reserving white areas for the flowers. Notice the accumulations of blue wash from the background, indicated by arrows in figure 71. These small smudges or drips, formed because of the vertical position of the drawing board actually bring out contrasts and help emphasize the forms and colors of the flowers.

67

68

69

71

72

Fresquet continues to reserve white, blank spaces for the flowers while drawing and painting in the leaves behind the bunch of white daisies in the lower right. "Tell your readers not to worry about drawing the exact form of the flower, petal by petal, when they are saving blank spaces; tell them that the important thing is that the watercolor be fresh, spontaneous, and true to their impression of what they see."

We take this lesson to heart.

Resolution of form and color

If we look at the result of the present phase of painting (fig. 77) and compare it to the previous phase (page 25, fig. 71), it seems as though Fresquet has done quite a bit of work. Certainly the vase has become a three-dimensional form. But as for the flowers, the most important work was completed as soon as the white spaces were saved. The central grouping of orange flowers, the forms and dirty green colors of the leaves and stems, the daisy buds extending into the sienna ground to the right—all these were there before. The only new addition is the yellow color of the flowers in the upper right, the pink spots defining the carnations, the corollas and shadows painted in over the saved white spaces of the daisies —especially noticeable in the top two— and the red of the top flower. Fresquet went to great pains to render this red flower with successive layers of color, waiting until each layer dried before applying the next. Also notice that this red flower, the yellow flowers, the carnations, and the white daisies are almost perfectly finished and appear just as they do in the final version (page 29, fig. 79).

There are three details about this phase that I'd like you to note.

First, Fresquet (like many other professionals) sometimes dilutes, erases, and paints with his fingers. In figure 73 we see him spreading out or "diffusing" the pink of one of the carnations.

Second, the transparent quality of watercolors makes it possible to blend colors by superimposing one over another. For example, Fresquet uses clear sienna to paint a plate over the grayish blue background. The blue ground color shows through and changes the original sienna to dark sienna (fig. 74).

73

74

75

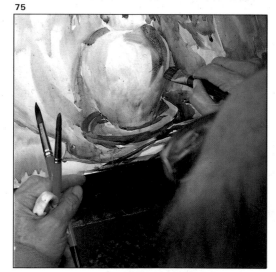

Fig. 73. At times the fingers themselves can be used to paint, dilute, tone down, or erase a color.

Fig. 74. As a transparent medium, watercolor permits blending of colors by layering one over another. Here Fresquet obtains a dark sienna by painting a wash of lighter raw sienna over a blue background.

Fig. 75. Fresquet renders the volume of the vase with a wash of warm gray —a mixture of ultramarine blue and burnt umber— that he will modulate to show the effects of light and shade.

Fig. 76. Synthesizing when drawing and painting, rather than worrying about every little detail and the exact form of every petal, is the hallmark of a good painter.

Fig. 77. The next to the last phase: The drawing, the color, the contrast, and the color harmony have all been resolved. Only a few final touches are still needed.

77

76

Third, the cloth behind the ceramic jar in the original setup is a relatively light blue. Fresquet, however, has not hesitated to reinterpret this part of what he sees in order to bring out the contrast in color and form between the ground and the ceramic vase.

Then Fresquet starts to put in the final modeling and sketched touches on the vase... but this brings us to the very last phase, which we are going to talk about next.

Finishing the painting

Fig. 78. Fresquet renders the patterns and colors of the ceramic vase by painting directly on the picture without having previously sketched anything.

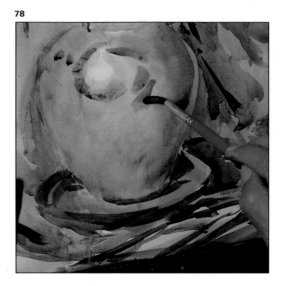

78

First the ceramic vase, the patterns and colors that decorate the vase, then the top red flower, then a few touches to the central cluster of orange flowers, next the two carnations in the bottom right corner...

Then we have arrived at the final phase in which the artist scrutinizes, assesses, adds a leaf here and a smudge there, darkens another area, exaggerates a contrast to emphasize an outline. It is in this final phase that Fresquet works slowly, looking over and observing his work repeatedly. As Picasso said, "You want to be painter? Observe. You can never observe what you have around you enough."

Last of all, Fresquet signs his work in the lower left corner, the darkest area of the painting. "I think that a signature shouldn't be overly noticeable," he says. "If the picture is of interest, the viewer will look for and find the signature. If it isn't..."

Fresquet cleans out his brushes, carefully squeezing them dry with a rag and leaving them in a can with the bristles sticking up. He closes the watercolor box.

"Don't you clean the palette?" I ask him.

The answer is a rapid and forceful, "No. I like to paint with dirty water and I prefer a dirty palette with leftover paints—usually grays, browns, and neutral colors that I mix in with the bright colors to try to achieve better color harmony and a consistent range of colors."

Fig. 79. A mere two hours have been sufficient for Fresquet to paint his picture from start to finish. It is a good example of composition, color harmony, and the skill and technique necessary for working in watercolor. This painting allows us to share Fresquet's interpretation of the setup and it is a fine example of its genre.

79

Jordi Segú: A very skilled watercolorist

Jordi Segú is a teacher with a degree in fine arts, a graphic artist, and a very skilled painter with various exhibitions to his name. He knows the techniques of watercolor painting so well that he draws and paints with incredible facility and speed. He seems to be unaware of having any special talent, as though just anyone could pick up a brush and paint with watercolors.

80

81

82

83

Fig. 80. Jordi Segú, a graphic artist and water-colorist, is going to develop a watercolor painting that manages to be simultane-ously modern and classical in style.

Figs. 81 to 83. These are materials that Jordi Segú usually uses —an assort-ment of twenty-four pan watercolors in a metal box. (It's possible to remove the color tray and then use the large subdivided enamel palette for dissolving and mixing.) He uses three sa-bles brushes —numbers 6, 8, and 14— as well as a soft lead pencil, a rag, water, and a wide-mouth jar like the one in figure 82.

The setup and an initial sketch

The setup is a bouquet of flowers in a simple ceramic vase. On the table from left to right, we can see a salt shaker, a coffee cup with a spoon and saucer, a red wax candle in a glass holder, a sugar bowl, and two apples.

Segú begins with a small sketch of 11 inches × 7 inches (28 cm × 18 cm). Notice how our guest artist has omitted some of the objects in the model. "Yes, I've left out the salt shaker and the sugar bowl," he explains, because this allows me to place the apples more toward the center."

Now study and observe for yourself the technique developed by Segú in this sketch, which took him exactly 14 minutes to complete. Note the few, precise brushstrokes he's used to paint the orange flowers, the saved white space for the lilies, and the halo around the bouquet, which shows how the

84

Fig. 84. The setup consists of a bouquet of flowers, a gray vase, and some typical objects on a tabletop. Everything is illuminated by backlighting.

Figs. 85 and 86. Figure 85 is a representation of the final painting. Figure 86 is Jordi Segú's initial sketch based on the setup with a dark background, but it eliminates some of the objects on the table.

85

images themselves appear to glow because of the backlighting. Also notice how appropriately he's represented the pink roses with just a few strokes that express their concrete form.

86

Jordi Segú's works

87

88

89

90

Figs. 87 to 90. Segú paints with both watercolors and oils, though he tends to prefer painting with watercolors "because of the ease and speed of the medium. It's possible to begin and complete a painting in one session that almost never takes more than two or three hours." We can admire Segú's versatility in such diverse subjects as landscape, seascape, nude, and still life.

Segú begins with a well-defined drawing

91

92

Segú now begins to draw with a soft-lead mechanical pencil on a pad of heavy-grain Arches or Canson watercolor paper, 10 inches × 14 inches (26 cm × 36 cm). His quick sketch is within view, the setup is in front of him, and his drawing board is inclined a few degrees, resting on his lap and leaning against the edge of the table where the setup is placed.

You can see the finished drawing in the adjoining illustration. It's a light linear sketch that's very detailed. It has no shading—the color will give it the shading. But already, by itself, the drawing has charm and merit. "It's not common to use such a thorough sketch," I point out. "Why have you made it so detailed?"

Segú finishes drawing the apples and answers firmly, "For some people, this kind of detailed drawing can be a constraint that doesn't allow any freedom. For me, this detailed drawing represents the opportunity to paint with more freedom later."

Undoubtedly he has a point.

"I agree with you. Are you going to paint a dark background?"

"No. This dark background doesn't really please me. I think it's not appropriate for a modern watercolor painting of flowers.

I'd say a uniformly dark studio background like this is something that belongs to the past. I'm going to try a light, luminous background that's in harmony with the theme and the medium: flowers in watercolor."

He has another valid point.

Figs. 91 and 92. Jordi Segú works on his drawing with the setup in front of him; the study he completed a few minutes ago is next to the drawing. Segu's detailed drawing offers a perfect scale of dimensions and proportions that, as he explains, allow him to paint with greater ease and freedom.

The background: Controlled and quick-drying

93

Segú begins the upper part of the background with a very light blue wash that gradually modulates to violet, gray-green, and salmon in different areas. The colors are subdued, but they determine the form of the bouquet already. They're light colors with a lot of water, which makes it necessary to lift up the drawing pad as if it were a board and put it in a horizontal position so the wash won't run. Since it takes a while to dry, Segú blows hot air from a hair dryer onto it, a method that many watercolorists use.

94

95

96

Figs. 93 to 97. Various stages of the painting. Segú ignores both the setup and his previous study by using a background done in light colors.

97

When the initial wash is dry, Segú paints a new layer of darker blue in the upper part of the painting, and a more intense color on the lower part of the painting that's next to the edge of the table.

Then, with a few confident brushstrokes, he paints the cup, the saucer, and the spoon, leaving them practically finished. In figure 98, notice how Segú keeps his drawing pad in a horizontal position to avoid trickling washes, and how he cleans and wipes off the brush with the rag he always keeps in his left hand. Then, with precise strokes that almost determine the form of the object, he paints the candle holder with vermilion and without hesitation resolves the color and form of the apples.

It's a pity you can't see the simple yet well-thought-out way Segú paints the shapes and forms we see. To paint the candle holder, the apple, or any of the objects in the painting. Segú first fills his brush with the appropriate color. He pauses with the brush a short distance from the area he's going to paint. Then with a kind of nervous back-and-forth motion as if he's calculating the precise movements of the brush, he first looks at the setup, then at the paper —again he looks at the setup and the paper— and then he flings the wash and the color onto the object, painting, diluting, absorbing, coloring, and evaluating at the same time. It's really a sight to see Segú painting!

98

99

100

Figs. 98 to 100. Segú paints on a pad of paper on a wooden drawing board that's inclined about 30 degrees. Often Segú lifts up the drawing pad and works on a less inclined or horizontal position. This enables him to control the brushfuls of wash so that they dry better. It also prevents drips from running down the page. Segú almost always keeps a rag available in his left hand for absorbing water and cleaning off his brush. (See fig. 98.)

Resolving the "holes" and saved blank spaces

Figs. 101 to 103. Segú resolves shapes and colors in an extraordinarily quick way. He begins and finishes painting the cup and saucer, the candle and the red container, the apples, and so on, in very few minutes. Then he begins to paint the bouquet of flowers, filling in the "holes" or blanks left between them, with "the idea of solving definitely the color of flowers, the color harmony of the bouquet, according to the color harmony of the objects on the table," he says.

In the third stage of the painting, which is shown on these two pages, Segú has only to paint the vase to finish the bottom half of the painting completely.

Segú has already painted the yellow apple by starting on the left with a light green ochre and adding some wet brushfuls of orange ochre. In the illuminated area at the top of the apple, wash and color are absorbed, leaving subtle gradations of tone. Finally Segú adds a touch of dark greenish yellow on the edge of the shaded area. He always paints with a wet brush on top of already wet brushstrokes. To resolve the

101

102

103

gradation of color as in the apple, in the background, or (as we'll see) in the flowers, Segú uses raw cotton. It's a technique that permits rapid absorption, while controlling the intensity of the color and hue.

The artist continues by filling in the "holes," the spaces that remain between the flowers. He uses a dark cobalt blue mixed with Payne's gray. Then he paints the vase with a mixture of ultramarine blue and carmine. He blends and diffuses the colors with his brush and a ball of raw cotton.

Finally he begins the flowers, starting with the orange chrysanthemum. This is part of the last stage, which you'll see on the following page.

Figs. 104 to 106. Everything is ready now to begin painting the flowers. The colors have to be filled in and contrasted, using the tones of the background and the other parts of the picture as a reference.

104

105

106

The finished painting

Figs. 107 to 111. Segú paints now with clear colors and washes that come almost directly from the pan. First he paints the lilies of the top section with a few sure strokes. Next he paints the roses and the red flower below. He paints alla prima, with a single layer of paint, and succeeds in achieving a fresh, spontaneous style. Then Segú intensifies the upper background to contrast with the white of the lilies in the upper left. Segú finishes the painting by signing it.

The adjoining illustrations show the last steps that finish the painting. Segú has spent 1 hour and 25 minutes.

It's enviable to be able to paint alla prima (in one session). The first layer of color defines, and at the most, a second layer adds form and volume. Segú's approach has yielded a harmony of luminous color and a feeling of spontaneous grace. These qualities are so important for a good watercolor painting.

Our congratulations, Segú!

107

108

109

110

111

Carmen Freixas: A specialist in painting flowers in watercolor

112

113

114

We're pleased to be able to include Carmen Freixas in this book on painting flowers in watercolor. She's a specialist in this field, with paintings in important collections and exhibitions. She's won first prizes and other awards for the artistic quality of her work. On these pages we show a sampling of her floral paintings.

Figs. 112 to 118. Carmen Freixas, an artist specializing in painting flowers in watercolor, appears here with some of her works. The way she interprets and composes a painting shows her truly original style. Look at figure 114. Carmen Freixas painted this work in collaboration with her husband, a specialist in illustration and figure painting in watercolors.

115

116

117

118

Freixas/Casamitjana: A unique artistic duo

120

119

Carmen Freixas and Luis Casamitjana, husband and wife, are professional artists. She is a watercolorist of flowers, and he is an outstanding professional in the field of illustration. Of course they live in the same house, and they have separate studios to work in. Casamitjana's is shown at the bottom of the page (fig. 122) and Freixas's is shown at the top (fig. 120). Look at the foreground of the photo of her studio. The kind of easel she uses has a wide inclinable board that functions as a table and allows her to paint with the paper at an angle. You can also see the small table where she lays out her supplies, and at the back, another small table that holds the vase and flowers that Freixas will paint.

Freixas and Casamitjana have had joint exhibitions with paintings like figure 121 on this page and figure 114 on page 40, in which he paints a motif, usually figures, and she paints the flowers. It's a perfect combination, a unique artistic duo that succeeds because of quality and sensitivity, always present in Carmen Freixas's paintings of flowers.

Figs. 119 and 120. Carmen Freixas is painting in her studio —the room shown in the accompanying illustration. Besides the paintings on the walls, in the foreground there's the small table and easel she usually uses, and in the background, the flowers she's going to paint.

121

122

Figs. 121 and 122. Luis Casamitjana, Freixas's husband, has his own studio in the same home. Here he draws and paints illustrations and occasionally collaborates with his wife, painting figures in works like the one we can see in figure 121.

The preliminary study and the setup

123

124

125

In Carmen Freixas's studio, in addition to the setup, there's a half-finished study of daisies and marigolds in an arrangement similar to today's bouquet. She explains, "Yesterday I bought these daisies and marigolds, and I painted this study to analyze the composition and form."

"But the arrangement of flowers isn't exactly the same," I interrupt.

"Of course not. I don't paint exactly what I see in the model. I always try to interpret a painting in my own way. For example, in the model there's a dark green vase and I'm thinking of painting the flowers without a vase. Looking at the model, the obvious way to paint it would be in a vertical format— but I've used a horizontal format in the study."

I interrupt her again. "Yes, and the flowers aren't the same. Did you paint them from memory?"

"Yes and no. I have the setup in front of me so I have a concrete reference for the form and color. But then I've painted so many flowers that it isn't a problem to paint them from memory, or in a different position, or larger or smaller, adding flowers or taking some away."

Freixas further explains her study. "I almost always do a sketch before I begin the

painting, and the painting is almost never the same as the sketch. In this one I thought about the flowers in the center with a light background. Now, though, I think it's better to darken the background to contrast and enliven the yellow and white of the daisies and marigolds."

Now she organizes the materials she needs to begin painting: a sheet of thick-grain Fabriano paper 20 inches × 14 inches (50 cm × 35 cm), three sable paintbrushes (numbers 10, 12, and 14), a flat brush 1 inch (2½ cm) wide; and two boxes and palettes of watercolors, which we'll describe on the following page.

Figs. 123 to 125. On the left is the sketch Freixas painted earlier as a study for the painting she's going to begin. The setup is on the right. It's a bouquet of white daisies and yellow marigolds. Shown below is one of the palettes Carmen Freixas uses. We'll comment on it and her other materials on the following page.

The drawing and the colors

126

127

Using a mechanical pencil with soft lead, Freixas interprets the bouquet of flowers in her own way, in an oval shape rather than in a circle, as it is in the setup. With only a few lines, she indicates the placement of some flowers and leaves that will determine the composition of the painting. (See the drawing in fig. 127.)

Next Freixas gets the colors ready. She uses a typical modern selection that includes lemon yellow, dark cadmium yellow, cadmium orange, vermilion, carmine, dark green, emerald green, dark yellow green, cobalt blue, sky blue, ultramarine blue, yellow ochre, and raw sienna. It's important to realize that Carmen doesn't use black, Payne's gray, or dark browns like burnt sienna or Vandyke brown.

Freixas's main palette has compartments, and she paints with creamy watercolors in tubes (fig. 128). She also uses an extra palette to mix and prepare colors (fig. 125 on page 43). Carmen explains, "Using two palettes lets me repeat colors, such as the carmine. I have a clean carmine for brushstrokes of precisely that color or to mix with light colors like yellow. Then I have another space with a dirty carmine I use to mix dark or dirty shades."

Figs. 126 and 127. Carmen Freixas's drawing is a linear outline of some flowers and leaves. It serves to position the elements of the painting. Figure 127 shows her interpretation and composition of the setup. She places it horizontally rather than vertically and eliminates the vase, making the flowers the sole focus of the painting.

Fig. 128. Carmen paints with creamy watercolors in tubes, using a palette with compartments and an additional palette (shown in fig. 125 on the preceding page). Notice that Carmen repeats some colors on her palettes —the carmine for example. "I have a dirty carmine available for mixing," she explains, "and a clean carmine to apply directly to the painting."

128

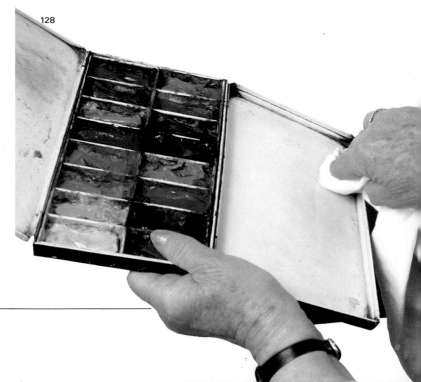

The way Carmen Freixas paints

129

130

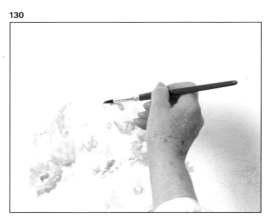

131

132

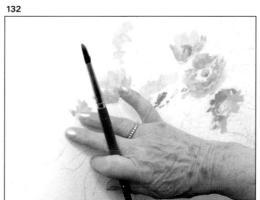

Figs. 129 to 132. As you can see in the illustrations, Freixas holds her brush in different positions depending on what form she's painting. She uses both wide and narrow brush-strokes, and she sometimes changes the direction of the stroke. In figure 132 see for yourself how she sometimes paints with her finger, using it to extend or dilute color, or even to draw with it.

Fig. 133. Freixas's interpretation of this painting begins to appear in profile. The bouquet fills all the horizontal space and the flowers in the center of the painting have the main role.

133

Painting with saved blank spaces

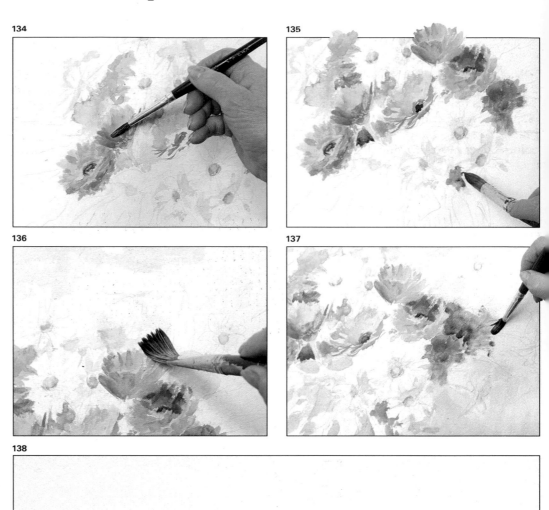

Figs. 134 to 138. The yellow marigolds can be painted directly, as if the artist were painting with opaque colors. Freixas resolves their form and color by superimposing dark over light, going from less color to more. Figure 137 and especially figure 138 correspond to the third stage of the painting. Here we can take note of the first saved white spaces that will eventually outline the white daisies.

The marigolds are yellow; the daisies are white. The marigolds can be painted directly with yellow or orange, on white paper, but the daisies have to be painted in negative. This means painting what's behind the flowers, whatever outlines their form, but keeping some space blank. Actually a watercolorist does more drawing than painting to create the petals of daisies.

"Saved blank space is essential in my paintings," Freixas says. "I almost always paint light flowers against dark backgrounds. I am used to seeing the opposite form of the shapes, the spaces that remain behind or between one form and another."

See for yourself the pictures on these two pages the laborious artistic process Carmen Freixas goes through to bring her flowers to life.

Figs. 139 to 141. Carmen Freixas is a true expert in saving white spaces in order to paint in negative. She shapes and outlines forms like the petals of the daisies in figure 140 or the vaguer pale shapes visible in figure 141, the fourth stage of the painting. By now the main part of the painting already has contrasts; it highlights the foreground. Carmen Freixas emphasizes, "To paint in watercolor, I believe it's necessary to see the shapes as they're defined by the background, to see them through the spaces between the forms."

139

140

141

Further developing the composition

Figs. 142 to 152. This sequence of photos reveals the step-by-step development of the painting: Carmen Freixas's techniques for drawing, painting, contrasting, and resolving. Study the development of each section of the painting. For example, compare figures 142, 143, 144, and 146 with the corresponding parts of figure 148 in the next to the last stage. Also compare figures 145 and 149, and 147 and 150. Finally, look at the enlarged final versions of figures 149 and 150 on page 50 (figs. 153 and 154).

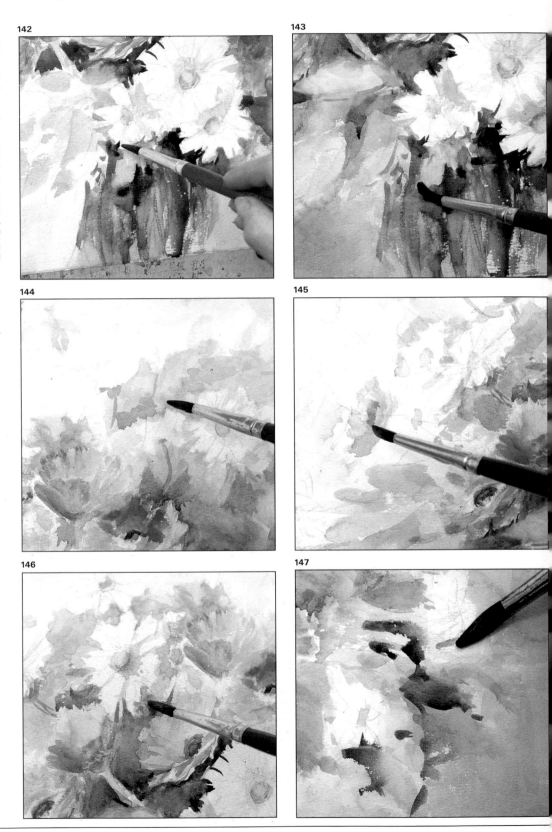

148

149

150

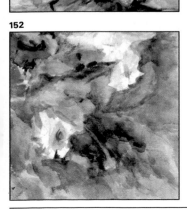

151

152

I'm standing behind Freixas observing how she completes the painting by adding shapes and colors, intensifying tones and shades, and reserving blank spaces. She's creating flowers she's invented that aren't in the setup and seem to appear as if by magic. She draws and paints at the same time, outlining a profile of a flower with a dark blue gray. She uses the same color to outline a leaf that appears below the flower, then changes the color of the leaf with a yellow-green tint, and puts the finishing touches on the flower with a stroke that forms the corolla.

To understand this process of painting, constructing, adding color here and there, and painting everywhere at the same time, look at the development illustrated in the photos (figs. 145 and 147). The same sections are seen in boxes in the fifth stage of the painting above (fig. 148). Study the process in this sequence of photos and in the finished painting (fig. 155 on pages 50 to 51).

The finished painting

Figs. 153 and 154. Carmen Freixas has finished the painting. These two enlarged details allow us to study her technique more closely —especially in conjunction with the pictures and text on pages 48 and 49.

Fig. 155. Here is Carmen Freixas's original painting of flowers. Its style is determined by three things: the resolution of forms, the composition, and the harmony of the colors. The artist's handling of these three factors results in her unique interpretation. The bouquet of marigolds and daisies in a glass vase was at hand, but Freixas used them as a simple reference that allowed her to paint her painting. She hasn't painted a still life with the requisite vase of flowers and complementary elements; she's painted flowers, only flowers. In the foreground, they're highlighted and well defined. Behind them are more flowers and in the background they become less and less concrete. Yet they are still flowers. It's a really original work that also includes an excellent range of softened colors —grays with brown and green tones— in perfect harmony.

Vicente B. Ballestar: An artist at work

156

157

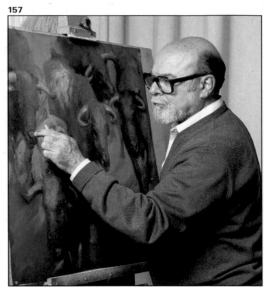

158

159

160

Vicente B. Ballestar is well known in Europe and America. An artist who has received many important awards and prizes, he paints both in oils and watercolors. His subject matter includes landscapes, seascapes, figures, animals, and still lifes. Samples of Ballestar's work appear on these pages. Also on this page is a picture of Ballestar's studio. It's located in an old apartment that has a large balcony through which an abundance of light enters. This is where Ballestar works, surrounded by books, paintings, portfolios, easels—and flowers, the subject he's going to paint now in watercolor.

Figs. 156 to 160. Vicente B. Ballestar, an outstanding oil painter, watercolorist, and draftsman, will paint a watercolor of flowers for us. Ballestar is a consummate artist, extraordinarily skilled in the technique of watercolor painting. This is evident in the quality of the paintings reproduced on the following pages.

161

Figs. 161 and 162. Here are examples of Ballestar's abilities as a painter and draftsman. He's able to paint a human figure seen from a foreshortened angle —the most difficult view to draw and put into correct proportion. Below is a magnificent demonstration of Ballestar's instinct for color harmony.

162

Two daring sketches

163

Figs. 163 and 164. Ballestar draws exceptionally well. He can draw any subject perfectly. Here, he's mastered the difficulties in presenting animals in motion.

164

Mounting the paper in a frame

This is the setup: an ivory-colored cloth as the backdrop; in front of it, a bouquet of anemones, two glass jars with water in them, a white ceramic jar with blue decorations, and a pack of cigarettes.

Ballestar looks at the setup. "The difficulty of painting the glass jars because of their transparency and reflections attracts me as much as painting the bouquet of flowers."

Ballestar gets the paper ready to draw by laying it down to stretch it out and mount it on a frame like those normally used for oil painting. He explains that he prefers this method to the usual one of stretching the paper on a wooden drawing board. Here's how he does it:

First he puts the watercolor paper on the floor with the frame on top of it. He cuts the paper and adjusts it to size (fig. 166).

165

Fig. 165. The setup Ballestar's chosen will serve only as a simple reference. The effects of the light and shading will be interpreted in his personal way, as we shall see.

Figs. 166 to 170. Ballestar mounts his paper on a wooden frame like those used for canvas in oil painting. With these illustrations, we can follow this process.

166

167

168

169

170

With a sponge and clean water he dampens the surface of the paper (fig. 167). Then with the frame on top of the paper, he folds the paper over one side of the frame and fastens it with a tack (fig. 168). He stretches the paper and does the same on the opposite side, folding the paper over the corners (fig. 169). He continues stretching and fastening (fig. 170), until the paper is perfectly mounted.

Ballestar explains, "As you can see, the paper is perfectly stretched and the damp side is on the back, so I can begin to draw before the paper dries completely."

The drawing and the background

Ballestar's palette box for creamy watercolors in tubes has a series of compartments in which we can see the colors: lemon yellow, cadmium yellow medium, vermilion, carmine, burnt sienna, cobalt blue, ultramarine blue, yellow ochre, raw sienna, Vandyke brown, dark green, and sky blue. He has water in a ceramic bowl and four brushes: two flat brushes with synthetic bristles and two sable rounds, numbers 12 and 14.

Ballestar draws rapidly, rendering the containers in detail but merely sketching the bouquet of flowers. Ballestar is left-handed. Now with that masterful hand he begins to paint the background, reserving white space for the objects.

Take note of a few aspects of the background. The general color range is warm, but diversity of shades enriches the paint-ing. Ballestar also provides a contrast around the ceramic jar with a more intense tone that will highlight the white. He uses only one layer of wash and outlines the white spaces with it.

Notice that Ballestar paints with the paper and frame in an almost vertical position. He's painted the background using a flat 1-inch (2.5-cm) brush with synthetic bristles. (You can see it in fig. 176.)

171

172

Fig. 171. Ballestar paints with creamy watercolors in tubes, in a wide assortment of colors (see the text above). His palette has compartments. He uses a minimum of brushes: two sable brushes (numbers 12 and 14) and two flat brushes with synthetic bristles.

Fig. 172. In his drawing, Ballestar has placed the objects toward the left of the picture, repeating the asymmetrical composition of the elements in the setup. The drawing perfectly outlines the basic shapes of the glass jars, the ceramic jar, and the cigarette pack. He sketches the bouquet of flowers with much less detail.

173

174

Figs. 173 to 177. Ballestar's talents are evident in the facility with which he paints. Notice how he reserves the white spaces.

175

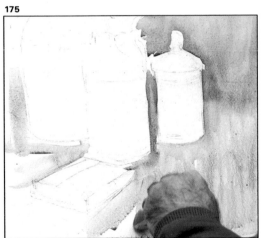

177

176

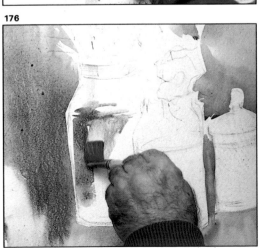

Painting the jars and flowers

Ballestar now begins to paint the setup and work with the white spaces reserved in the previous phase.

He begins with the water in the jars, delineating the bluish shadowed areas, the reflections, and the shapes we see through the transparent glass. He uses greens and dirty browns to paint the stems inside the large jar, but is careful to preserve the shine and reflections at the edges and top of the jar.

Still painting with a wide brush, Ballestar combines purple, cobalt blue, and carmine to begin the first flower: the anemone in the small jar. He uses a carefree stroke and paints the right side of the flower with a lighter color, then the rest with a darker tone. Quickly he cleans the wide brush and fills in with carmine to paint the anemone in the upper right. Then he partially cleans the brush and mixes what's left of the carmine with yellow and cobalt blue to create a dirty green, with which he forms some of the stems and leaves of the bouquet. Next he cleans the brush with water and paints the red anemone in the center of the bouquet with an almost uniform splotch. He continues with the blue-violet anemone in the upper left.

Here I feel obligated to ask Ballestar why he doesn't first paint all the red flowers and then all the blue ones.

"Productivity is at odds with art," he answers. "I'm not painting this in a series—first of all because I'm concerned with filling certain spaces, but mostly because painting the reds and carmines and then the blues and violets would create a uniformity and monotony of colors. Tell the readers to observe the different colors of the blue anemones in the third stage (fig. 181) to understand that my method will diversify and enliven the color."

178

179

Figs. 178 to 180. Ballestar now works in a completely concentrated way. He interprets the reflections of the glass jars in his own way, beginning to paint them with washes of neutral grays, blues, and browns. With a flat brush (fig. 180) he paints the foundations of the shapes and reflections. We see this in the reproduction of the second stage of the painting (fig. 178).

180

181

182

183

184

185

186

Figs. 181 to 186. In these illustrations, look at the forms and shapes Ballestar uses to arrive at the third stage of the painting (fig. 181). Already there's a sense of the finished product.

Details of finishing the painting

Ballestar now uses one of the round brushes to pull together and almost complete the bouquet. He paints practically from memory alone, consulting the setup occasionally only to confirm or compare colors. But the proportions, dimensions, and shapes of the flowers reflect Ballestar's interpretation. For example, he paints the daisies in the upper portion of the painting in different positions and larger than those of the actual bouquet. He takes advantage of the previously reserved white spaces and shapes the daisies with a light grayish blue wash. Notice how he's made all the flowers larger, including the yellow one.

In this general finishing up, Ballestar resolves several small details. He paints in the dark corollas of the anemones with a black made of ultramarine blue and carmine. He finishes some stems and leaves in the upper left, as well as the yellow centers of the daisies. He fills in small spots of color to create contrast and outline the shapes in the large glass jar. He also adds more leaves and stems.

Still painting with the number 12 sable round, Ballestar creates definitive shapes that correspond to the reflections within the small glass jar. With one brushstroke of dark color, he separates the small jar from the ceramic jar. Now, using a flat synthetic brush, he applies a coat of ivory to the ceramic jar and at the same time adds gradations of tone to portray its volume.

There's very little left to do in order to finish the painting. Ballestar now lights a cigarette, puts down the brushes and rag, and says, "I could finish painting the decorations on the ceramic jar, the pack of cigarettes, the daisies, and a few other details, but I want to work on form—outlining contrasts and accentuating color harmony. Why don't we leave the painting alone for a few minutes."

We go to another room in his studio and chat for a few minutes. It reminds me to mention the usefulness of stopping for a little while, no matter how short, in order to return to the painting with a clearer judgment of what's done and what's left to be done.

187

188

Figs. 187 to 195. At the fourth stage (fig. 195) the painting is almost finished, except for a few last-minute details and contrasts. Ballestar works in this phase with a number 12 round sable brush. In his right hand, he always keeps a damp cloth that he uses to remove water or wash from the brush (fig. 188). As he paints and draws, he creates colors and forms. By this stage the transparency, radiance, and reflections of the water and glass are almost completely captured. He's begun the finishing touches on the decorations of the ceramic jar, and the first brushstrokes that will shape the daisies in the upper part of the picture.

195

189

190

191

192

193

194

The range of colors in the finished painting

In another room of the studio, next to a good collection of art books, my conversation with Ballestar turns to the topic of color range and harmonization. Ballestar has occasionally taught painting and thus naturally has an opinion on these subjects.

"You'll agree that the subject of the painting determines the color range," he says as he leads me to the painting. "For example, the glass jars, the reflections and shine, the undefined color of the stems inside the water, call for a range of grays made of complementary mixes of ultramarine blue and yellow, green and carmine, blue and vermilion." He also uses siennas and browns that combine with the white paper to give an immense range of dirty colors, grays and neutrals. "They tend to be warm colors, wouldn't you agree?"

Yes, I agree. Ballestar has finished his lecture and now wants to demonstrate what he has just said. He looks at the painting, picks up the number 12 round, and mixes an almost black color from ultramarine blue, yellow, and Vandyke brown. With rapid, sure strokes, he paints a dark area behind the violet anemone in the upper right. Then he adds a daisy, develops the shapes of the other daisies, and intensifies the color of the stems and leaves. He lightens the color and then repaints the background of the upper left part of the picture. Next he cleans his brush, dampens the petal of the blue anemone, and then once again fills his brush, this time with a dark brown used to intensify or darken other areas. Afterward, he finishes the white anemone and returns to the blue one with a loaded brush. He opens up the flower with a blue lighter than the original blue of the flower in the bouquet.

Ballestar doesn't stop. He's in a fever of involvement with everything in the painting. He always paints standing. He steps back from the painting, adjusts his perspective, and then goes from one end of the painting to the other, finishing flowers, leaves, stems, the ceramic jar, and the cigarette pack. Then he pauses.

"I'm going to finish the glass jars." He lights another cigarette and mixes a dark grayish color. Then, using variants of blue gray, gray sienna, and green gray, he defines the water level, intensifies dark areas, and gives form to spots and shapes. This is how he finishes the painting.

He's given us a good, practical example of painting flowers in watercolors.

Fig. 196. This is the other room in Ballestar's studio. Apart from using the table in the foreground, the artist basically uses this room to draw. We can see one of the artist's "vices," as he refers to it: He buys art books and he has a good collection in his studio.

Fig. 197. In the adjoining illustration, Ballestar intensifies the color of the upper background by blurring the grayish brown with the reserved space. Then he paints the daisy in the upper section.

Fig. 198. Watercolor is a medium with practically limitless possibilites— but it demands skill and special techniques because of its transparency and because the color white is the white of the paper. Ballestar's magnificent finished painting is an excellent example of the potential of this medium and of the skills required to bring out that potential.

196

197

198

Contents